WHAT'S THE JOKE, BEETLE BAILEY

Here's another in the happy series of books based on one of the most famous comic strips in the country. Once again the madcap inmates of Camp Swampy valiantly strive to overcome their own ineptitude—and succeed in delighting us on every page.

Mort Walker again gives us a barrel of laughs in his marvelous cartoons concerning the most unprofessional soldier in the Army!

Beetle Bailey Books

WHAT'S THE JOKE,

beetle bailey®

by Mort Walker

CHARTER BOOKS, NEW YORK

WHAT'S THE JOKE, BEETLE BAILEY

A Charter Book / published by arrangement with
King Features Syndicate, Inc.

PRINTING HISTORY
Charter edition / March 1987

ISBN: 0-441-05279-7

Charter Books are published by The Berkley Publishing Group,
200 Madison Avenue, New York, New York 10016.
PRINTED IN THE UNITED STATES OF AMERICA

7-7

ISN'T IT KINDA DUMB TO MAKE BEETLE THE COMPANY RUNNER, SIR?

LOOK AT IT THIS WAY, SARGE...

8-2

...HOW FAST DO YOU WANT HEADQUARTERS TO KNOW WHAT'S GOING ON HERE?

SHREWD